STEVE *the* Christmas ELF

Buster Books

Edited by Imogen Currell-Williams

Designed by Jack Clucas

Cover design by John Bigwood

First published in Great Britain in 2021 by Buster Books,
an imprint of Michael O'Mara Books Limited, 9 Lion Yard,
Tremadoc Road, London SW4 7NQ

W www.mombooks.com/buster f Buster Books 🐦 @BusterBooks 📷 @buster_books

A CIP catalogue record for this book is available from the British Library.

ISBN: 978-1-78055-712-0

1 3 5 7 9 10 8 6 4 2

This book was printed in August 2021 by Leo Paper Products Ltd,
Heshan Astros Printing Limited, Xuantan Temple Industrial Zone,
Gulao Town, Heshan City, Guangdong Province, China.

Written by

Billy Dunne

Illustrated by

Ben Whitehouse

For William and Katie – BD

For Yvonne and Timmy – BW

Steve the **MAGIC** Christmas elf
was working through the night,

Creating planes for girls and boys
by dimming candlelight.

When all at once he had a thought
no elf had thought before,

A thought so deep it made him **DROP**

his presents to the floor.

"We can't be sure that girls exist,
or even little boys."

"I think that Santa made them up, and **PINCHES** all the toys!"

"There are far too many sleeping kids
to visit in one night."
And so he **SNUCK** aboard the sleigh
to see if he was right.

He **BLASTED** over continents ...

... and oceans in between.

He **THUNDERED**

through the winter's night,
and turned a sickly green.

He landed on a sloping roof
and **DASHED** across the snow.

Then climbed inside a chimney stack
and worked his way **BELOW**.

And then at last he felt the tug

of fingers grabbing toes.

A girl called May had dragged him out –

in disbelief, he **FROZE.**

"My goodness me! A little girl! You really do exist.
But tell me why you look so sad?"

"I'm on the
NAUGHTY LIST."

"My brother asked to share my toys,
I wouldn't let him play,"

"And now there won't be any gifts

for me on Christmas Day."

Above they heard the sleigh bells **RING**.

"You need to go," May said.

But Steve preferred to stay behind,

and comfort her instead.

"You must be **KIND** to girls and boys,
that's how it's best to be."

"To get me home you'll have to learn
to share your toys with me."

May shared without a moment's pause,

and didn't once complain.

And from her fancy toys Steve made ...

...A MAGIC
AEROPLANE!

They hugged goodbye
and off he flew,
"I won't forget you, May!"

HE BARREL-ROLLED...

...THEN LOOPED-THE-LOOP

AND LANDED ON THE **SLEIGH!**

And as for May, she learned to share
that snowy Christmas Eve.

And by her bed there sat a gift,

from Santa Claus and Steve.